Professor Featherbottom was born and raised on a small, uncharted island formed thousands of years ago during the eruption of an ancient volcano in the far, far reaches of the South Pacific Ocean. It was here in this now sleepy volcano that he learned to draw by sketching the many exotic birds and animals that soon came to see him as a trusted friend and protector. He learned to understand their sounds and their language and, through them, he learned to care for all creatures.

Here he was raised by his mother, the last of a noble and peaceful race that once graced these remote volcanic islands, on the stories and lessons passed down to her over countless generations by her people. When he grew up he left this island paradise to bring these stories and the lessons of his childhood to the world. "The Last Rainbow" is just such a story.

Enjoy and may the wisdom of the world soon find you in its heart.

ISBN: 978-0-578-51365-2
Library of Congress Control Number: 2019910246

To Alex and Valentina

THE LAST
RAINBOW

FERGUS awoke from his bed with a start. Today was his birthday! But it wasn't just *any* birthday.

Today was Fergus' 100th birthday! And of all birthdays, a leprechaun's 100th birthday was the most special of all! For on a leprechaun's 100th birthday they got their *very own* Rainbow.

Now we all know that every leprechaun has a Pot o' Gold. But until a leprechaun gets their own Rainbow, they can never hide this Pot o' Gold. For only at the end of a Rainbow can such a treasure be concealed.

But how does a leprechaun get a Rainbow on their 100th birthday? Why, they each pick their Rainbow at the Annual Rainbow Celebration held in the highest hills of Tara.

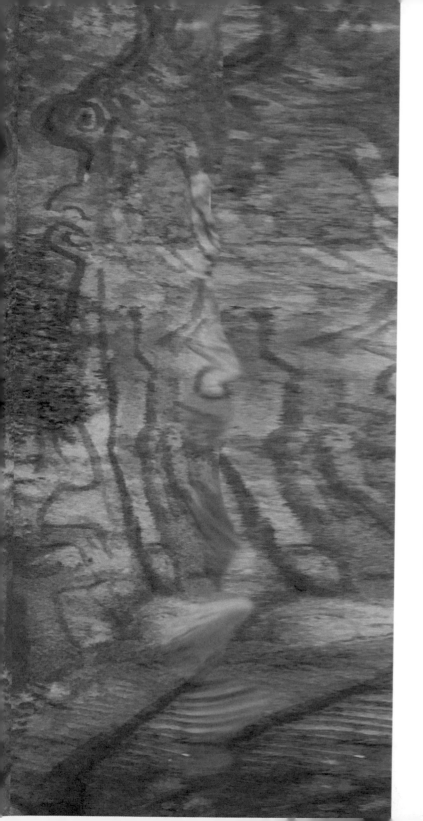

So Fergus rushed out of his cozy home burrowed into the green, grassy knoll, through the rustic wooden gate and down the well worn path to the Forest of Ballyannan.

For there in the Forest of Ballyannan lived the wise old King of the Owls, King Scrimclaw, who alone knew the exact location of the Annual Rainbow Celebration.

Fergus hurried down the dusty path, worn by the shoes of generations of leprechauns before him, to the center of the Forest.

The animals of the Forest called out to Fergus as he hurried down the path, for they all loved this cheerful little leprechaun. "Happy Birthday, Fergus" they called out, but Fergus hardly heard their well-wishes.

For his mind was elsewhere. He couldn't be late to the Annual Rainbow Celebration! You see, the first leprechaun to arrive at the Annual Rainbow Celebration got the first pick out of all the Rainbows.

And Fergus, of all days, had overslept this morning.

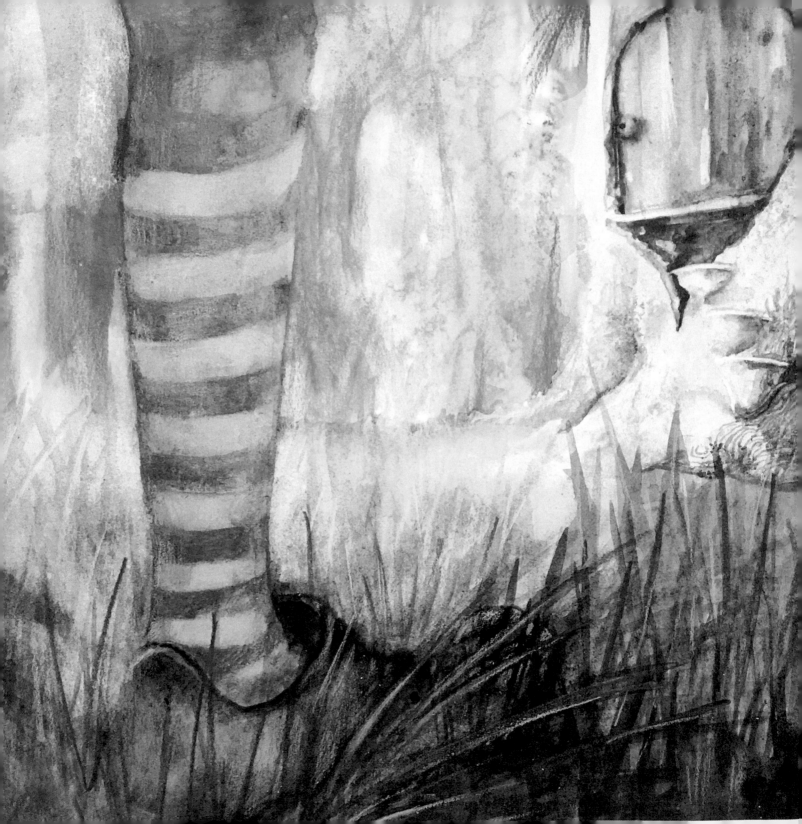

He huffed and he puffed and he hurried down the path deep into the Forest until he came to the highest and mightiest tree. This must be the home of the wise and noble King Scrimclaw!

Like all leprechauns before him, Fergus knocked on the tree and chanted the magic words,

"Lo and behold,
I'm 100 years old!
Great King of the Owls,
Please help hide my Gold!"

And then he waited, silently, at the foot of the Great Tree.

And he waited.

And he waited.

And just when Fergus thought he could wait no longer, he heard a rustle from above.

Out from a large hole in the trunk of the Great Tree came an owl as white as snow, with only the very tip of his beak, colored black as night, to offset his fair, downy coat. It was the wise and noble King Scrimclaw, Ruler of the Owls!

The King was larger than any owl Fergus had ever seen and his eyes, while half-closed as if roused from a long and restful sleep, shone bright as the sun.

There could be no mistaking the sparkle in these eyes. Within these eyes lay pools of the deepest wisdom. They were timeless. They were the eyes of a King.

"Hello, Fergus. I've been expecting you," yawned King Scrimclaw as he slowly opened his eyes. "I was wondering whether you were going to make it at all."

"I'm terribly sorry, Your Majesty!" replied Fergus. "Of all days, of all years, to oversleep, I did so today. Am I too late for the Rainbow Celebration?"

Kings Scrimclaw yawned again as he stretched, fluttering his large, majestic wings, all the while gazing intently at Fergus with his wise, thoughtful eyes. "This is your 100 year birthday, Fergus. You can never _miss_ your Rainbow Celebration. Your Rainbow selection, however, may be ... more limited when you arrive."

"But arrive you will, and the Rainbow you choose will hide your Pot o' Gold always," said the King. He leaned forward on his branch and said in a whisper, "So you must take care to _choose wisely._"

Then, in his slow, unhurried manner King Scrimclaw gave Fergus the secret map to the Annual Rainbow Celebration and the instructions that he would need. Fergus fidgeted with excitement as he tried to listen patiently to the words of the Great King.

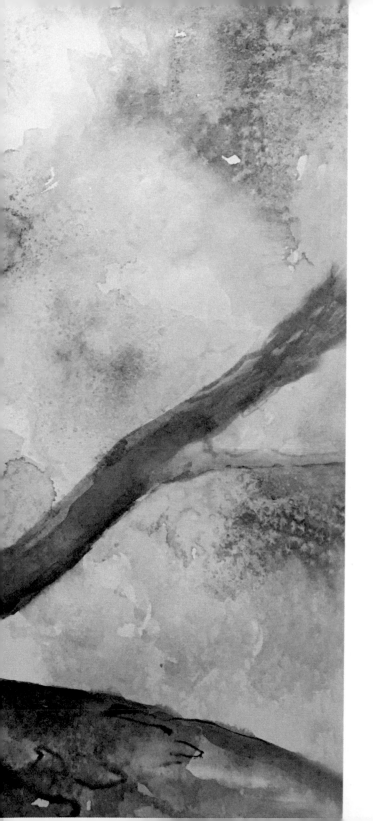

After what felt to Fergus like ages the King fell silent. Fergus politely thanked him, turned and started down the path towards the Rainbow Celebration. But as he did, he heard once more the wise and noble voice of King Scrimclaw,

"Remember, Fergus, the world always works as it should. Only time can show the wisdom of its path. Be patient, and all will be as it must."

He slowly turned toward his hole, and then stopped. Turning his great head back to Fergus he said,

"Sometimes, Fergus, it's what we think we are missing that makes us most special."

And with that, the Noble King winked, turned his head and slipped silently into his hole.

Fergus puzzled thoughtfully over the King's words as he started down the path. He sensed a deep meaning to the words, yet try as he might he could not seem to find it.

And as his excitement for the Rainbow Celebration returned he soon forgot about the King's words altogether.

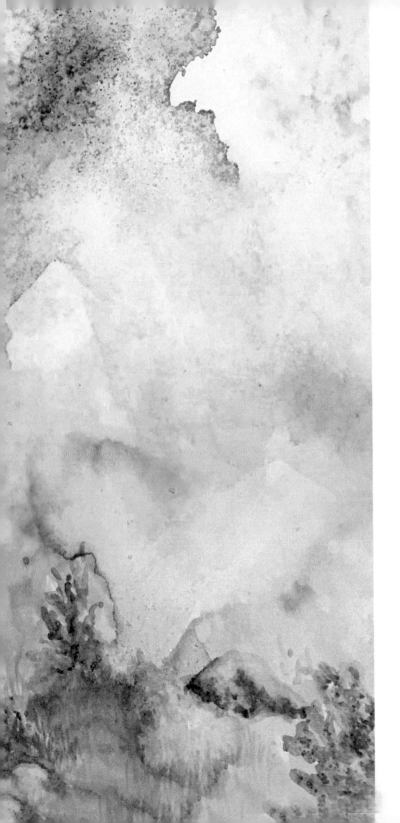

Over far away hill and dale, mountain and valley, Fergus hurried as he made his way to the Rainbow Celebration. Finally, at the crest of a high and rolling knoll he glimpsed a most amazing sight- the Annual Rainbow Celebration!

In the valley, as far as the eye could see, were Rainbows- beautiful, beautiful Rainbows, each a magnificent array of colors. There was purple, blue, green and yellow. There was orange and pink. And there was the most radiant red. It was unlike anything Fergus had ever seen! He could not imagine any place he would rather be.

And there were leprechauns everywhere, more leprechauns than he had ever seen before. They came in all shapes and sizes, every one in green. Some had beards and some did not, with hats both high and low. Some had pipes and some had canes. But each had the most beautiful buckles on their shoes and belt, glistening like stars on a clear, crisp night.

As he walked down among the throngs, he noticed that each leprechaun had a Rainbow, their own, beautiful Rainbow. Fergus hurried here and there, to and fro, searching for a Rainbow that didn't have a leprechaun. He couldn't find any! Not one. Could it be that he was too late?

"This can't be! This just can't be! There must be a Rainbow here for me!" thought Fergus.

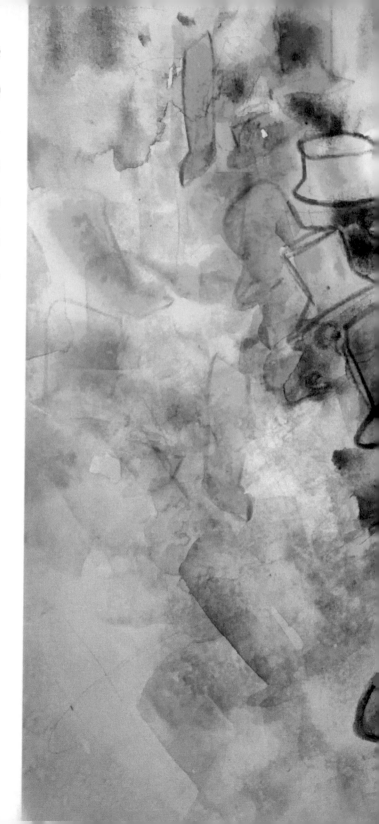

Just at that moment he spotted an old leprechaun carrying a long, long list scrolled out in a large pile at his feet. "This must be the Rainbow List, with all the Rainbows for all the leprechauns," thought Fergus. "My Rainbow must surely be there."

Fergus hurried to the old leprechaun and said, "Excuse me, Sir. My name is Fergus and today is my 100th birthday. Can you tell me where I can find my Rainbow?"

The old leprechaun squinted his eyes and puffed his pipe. He looked Fergus up and down, scratched his long, bushy beard and said, "My friend, you're too late. There are no more Rainbows. I'm sorry."

He puffed on his pipe again and looked down at the long list once more. As he got to the very bottom of the list he stopped, looked up and said,

"But wait! There _is_ one Rainbow left! Though warn you I must. This Rainbow is not like the others."

As Fergus' eyes followed the old leprechaun's gaze, he started and caught his breath.

There, standing alone at the edge of the valley was the Last Rainbow. It had purple, blue, green and yellow. It had orange and it had pink. But there was no red! The Rainbow was missing its red!

Fergus turned back to the leprechaun and said, "This can't be! There must be another Rainbow on your list. There must! Please look and you'll see!"

The old leprechaun sadly shook his head and puffed again on his pipe. "I'm sorry, my friend, there is no mistake. That is the Last Rainbow. There are no more." He rolled up his long list and slowly walked away, leaving Fergus sadly shaking his head. This was supposed to be the best day of his life, but for the first time Fergus was truly unhappy.

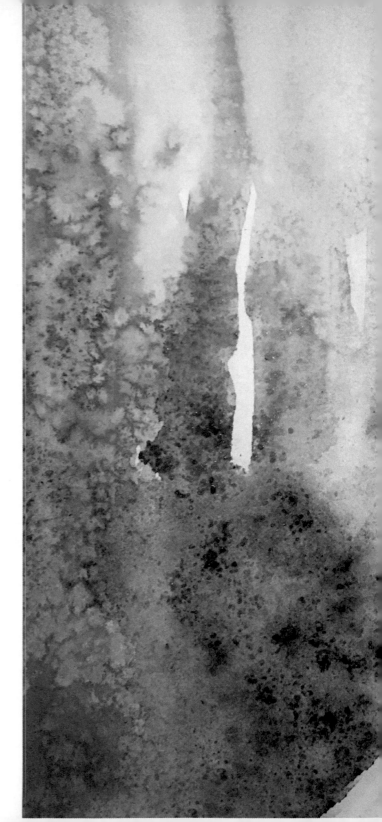

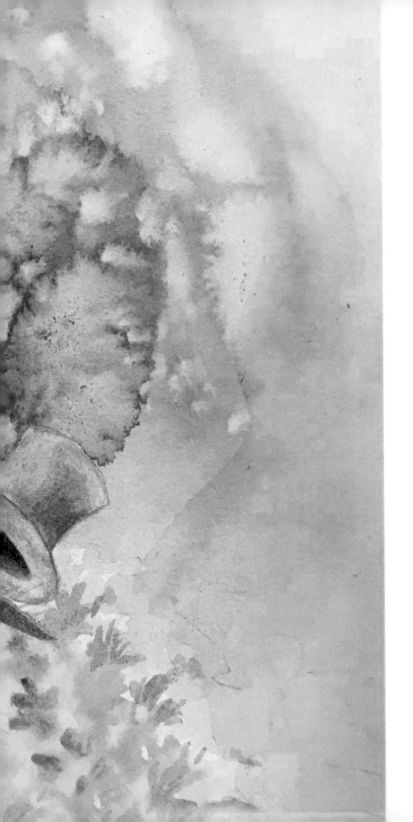

He walked to the top of the knoll and sat down. "I must be the most unlucky leprechaun of all. How could this be?" he thought. "There's only one Rainbow left, missing its red no less!" He thought back on the words of the wise and noble King Scrimclaw. The King had told him that he could never *miss* his Rainbow Celebration. It seemed to Fergus that maybe the King was not so wise after all.

Fergus thought again of what the King had told him,

"Sometimes, Fergus, it's what we think we are missing that makes us most special."

As he sat there feeling sorry for himself he wondered what the King could possibly have meant.

And as he reflected on this, Fergus looked down the knoll to the Rainbow Celebration. But this time, he noticed something. All of the Rainbows in the valley looked the same. In fact, they were all _exactly_ the same. Each Rainbow looked just like every other Rainbow.   Try as he might, Fergus could not tell the difference from one to another.

All except for one. One Rainbow, amongst all the others, stood out as it sat by itself at the edge of the valley. It was the Last Rainbow.

"Sometimes, Fergus, it's what we think we are missing that makes us most special."

Fergus finally understood what King Scrimclaw meant! As he dashed down the hill to the Last Rainbow, he realized that he wasn't the most _unlucky_ leprechaun. In fact, he was the _luckiest_ leprechaun of all. Fergus ran to the Last Rainbow and, catching his breath, gasped, "My name is Fergus. Would you, could you, be my Rainbow?"

The Rainbow sadly replied, "You don't want me to be your Rainbow, little leprechaun. Nobody wants me. I'm not like the other Rainbows. I have no red."

Fergus broke into a broad grin, the sun dancing off his bright, white teeth and said, "You're right, my friend. You are different from all the other Rainbows. But that's what makes you special. The most special Rainbow of all. And if you would be my Rainbow, you would make me the happiest of all the leprechauns."

The Last Rainbow looked up and his frown slowly faded. In its place rose the most brilliant, most colorful smile ever seen in Rainbow Valley. For the first time, the Last Rainbow didn't feel like he was different. For the first time, he didn't feel like the Last Rainbow. For he finally realized that he was special, the most special Rainbow of all.

And with that, the cheerful little leprechaun and the Rainbow with no red walked away together as the sun slowly set on Rainbow Valley.

The Last Rainbow hides Fergus' Pot o' Gold to this very day. And if you look very hard, and if you're very, very lucky, you may see the Last Rainbow, the one that has no red. And if you are one of the fortunate few to catch this magical sight, remember to make a very special wish. For it is only the Last Rainbow that can grant just such a wish.

Made in the USA
Middletown, DE
01 March 2022

61935073R00029